How Could They?

It had happened to several of her friends. In fact, half the kids in her class had parents who were divorced. But it hadn't happened to her family. Yet. And it still mustn't.

Sapphie thumped the pillow furiously then buried her head in it. Why were her parents putting her through this? And on the night before her birthday. How could they? Despite her black mood a little thrill still went through her at the thought of being a teenager.

She sat up and hugged her knees. All year looking forward to this moment and now it was spoilt.

Published by Evans Brothers Limited
2A Portman Mansions
Chiltern Street
London W1U 6NR

First published 2002

British Library Cataloguing in Publication Data
Vyner, Sue
How Could They?
1. Children's Stories
I. Title
823.9'14 [J]

ISBN 0 237 52421 X

Series Editor: Julia Moffatt
Designer: Jane Hawkins

Chapter One

Her parents were at it before they were hardly home from work. Strong, bitter words of argument.

Sapphie suddenly realised how long it had been since Dad'd rushed in and bear-hugged Mum like he used to, then grabbed hold of Sapphie and hugged her too.

Instead, as soon as they were together now, there was this animosity between them. And a simmering, seething smouldering feeling that made Sapphie feel sick.

It wasn't so much what they said. As how they said it.

'And where are you off to next? Paris? Milan?' Dad was saying to Mum now. His voice clipped and sharp. They didn't seem to care that Sapphie was listening. That was something else that was different.

'You know where I'm going next. I always keep you informed,' Mum said.

'Informed.' Dad spat the word out. 'Thanks a million.'

'Guys!' Sapphie said.

They stopped in their tracks. Then guilty smiles replaced the tight frowns on their faces.

'It's getting worse,' Sapphie told Becky at school the next morning. 'They can hardly keep a civil tongue in their heads at the moment.'

'*At the moment*,' Becky repeated. 'That's it Saph. They're just going through a bad patch. It will pass.' She shrugged.

Sapphie frowned. 'But it didn't used to be like this,' she insisted.

'Our house is always a battlefield,' Becky said. 'You're just not used to it.'

'And I prefer not to be used to it,' Sapphie said, wishing for a bit more sympathy from her best friend.

That night it was a repeat performance. Dad going on about Mum's imminent trip to Paris.

But he'd never minded about her trips before, Sapphie thought.

'And why is Max going this time?' Dad said. A strong note of jealousy in his voice.

Sapphie drew in her breath. So was that the problem? Was Dad jealous? Sapphie held her breath. Did Dad have reason to be jealous? She listened carefully.

'Max is my boss. He decides where he goes and what he does,' Mum said. 'He wants to be there this time. That's all.'

Dad didn't say anything to that. But it was his silence, now, that indicated his strong disapproval.

Suddenly he turned his back on Mum and concentrated his attention on Sapphie.

'Thirteen tomorrow,' he said. 'My little girl a teenager!'

Sapphie sighed. It had seemed like they'd forgotten about the huge milestone looming in her life. And after her looking forward to this birthday all year.

'You're not going to turn into a monster are you, pet?' Dad said and grabbed Sapphie playfully. 'We're not going to have to cope with a female Kevin from now on, are we?'

Sapphie wanted to laugh. But there was something about the monster bit that rang too true. Only her parents should look at themselves first.

In bed that night Sapphie felt herself getting more excited about her birthday. But then she heard another row erupt downstairs. She lay unwillingly listening to what it was about this time. And when she heard, she froze.

First, Dad went on about Mum going away. Again. And then about Max going with her. Again. It was almost word for word what they'd said before. But then it got much, much worse.

'We can't go on like this,' Mum suddenly shouted. 'Enough is enough. We may as well admit it. It's over!'

Sapphie tried to imagine Dad's face.

'We may as well go our own separate ways,' Mum shouted. Her words piercingly clear. 'A clean break. It's the only answer!'

'Right,' Dad retorted. 'If that's how you want it. A clean break it will be!'

Sapphie couldn't believe what she was hearing. She got up and hurried on to the landing. To see Dad appear below her in the hallway. He flung his coat on and dashed out of the door.

Sapphie ran back into her bedroom and threw herself on the bed.

It had happened to several of her friends. In fact, half the kids in her class had parents who were divorced. But it hadn't happened to her family. Yet. And it still mustn't.

Sapphie thumped the pillow furiously then buried her head in it. Why were her parents putting her through this? And on the night before her birthday. How could they? Despite her black mood a little thrill still went through her at the thought of being a teenager.

She sat up and hugged her knees. All year looking forward to this moment and now it was spoilt.

If they split up which one would leave, she wondered? Which one would stay? Which parent would claim *her*? She supposed that Mum'd have the house and she'd stay with her. That's how it usually happened, wasn't it?

Sapphie scowled. Well it wasn't fair then, was it? Because it was Mum'd said she wanted the break. 'It's the only answer!' she'd said.

So. Fair's fair. If Mum wanted a divorce, *she'd* have to leave wouldn't she? Sapphie drew in her breath sharply. Because then it would mean herself leaving home too, wouldn't it? And where would they go?

No sooner was she worrying about this problem than another one occurred to her. What if she didn't want to go with her mother?

As the enormity of it all struck her, Sapphie let out her breath slowly. How did anyone choose between their mother and their father?

She got out of bed and walked over to the window. Drew the curtains and looked out at the familiar view. It wasn't fair. She didn't want to choose. None of this was her fault. She folded her arms round herself and rocked gently. In all her life, Sapphie'd had no idea that anything could be as bad as this.

She slumped down in the chair by the window and stared out at the dark night sky...

Chapter Two

Sapphie was an only child. When she was little, she'd asked her parents why, and they'd said that when she was born their family was complete. Sapphie was all they wanted and needed. They were the perfect family. She grew up confident in that knowledge.

Mum was the most confident person Sapphie knew. Sapphie supposed that was why she was so good at her job. She was a textile designer and sold most of her designs abroad. Hence the visits to Paris, Milan, LA. 'Thank goodness for Kate,' she'd say when another trip was due. Kate being Mum's best friend, and always there for Sapphie when Mum was away. Sapphie would pop round and Kate would spoil her like mad. Just like Mum spoilt her.

And Dad. Dad worked in computers and was obsessive about his work. But despite all the long hours he worked, he adored his daughter, which meant he spoilt her too.

They *were* the perfect family. Didn't Becky envy Sapphie? Always telling her that she could have more or less what she wanted. Go more or less where she wanted. Sapphie had already been to places where some people might never go. America: Disneyland, the Grand Canyon, San Francisco; France: the south of France, Paris; Switzerland: skiing in the Alps. The list was endless. Dad and Mum both worked hard and said they deserved to play hard when they got the chance. And when they were holidaying, Sapphie always went with them.

Sapphie had a wardrobe full of up-to-date clothes that Becky would die for. Mum brought snazzy little items back for them both from her trips abroad. And she encouraged Sapphie to experiment with fashion and style. Mum was the most stylish mum of any mum Sapphie knew. But always in an understated way. Never in a way that would embarrass Sapphie. Sapphie loved her mother very much and was proud of her. She was proud when people said that with her short dark bouncy hair and wide smile she looked like her mum. She loved her father too. And was proud when people said she'd got his sense of fun.

Her family had been good together. Until recently.

Sapphie got back into bed and lay on her back staring up at the ceiling.

So how had it all come to this?

Sapphie couldn't remember the last time her parents had fooled around together like they used to. The fact was, they didn't any more. It was all snide remarks now. Carping and fault finding, and quarrels.

When had the quarrels started? And why hadn't she taken more notice of them? Why hadn't she done something about it to stop them?

But Dad must still love Mum, mustn't he? Mum must still love Dad, mustn't she? They always had before. How could they suddenly not love each other any more?

Then Sapphie squirmed. Didn't she read about this sort of thing happening all the time in the magazines which Mum devoured? Weren't there endless articles about doing your own thing? Getting out of bad relationships even if it meant leaving your family.

Sapphie shuddered. She was still in shock about it. All of it had seemed so – other people. Until now.

She turned onto her side and curled up tight.

Surely her parents would never divorce. Would they?

And tomorrow was her birthday.

Sapphie's future suddenly looked very bleak. And very scary. And suddenly, Sapphie didn't want to be a teenager. Not if it meant having to deal with things like this...

'I know you're a teenager now and all that,' Dad said, throwing a small package on the bed, 'but even teenagers wake up early on their birthday.' He sat down on the edge of the bed. Sapphie uncurled and grinned at him. Then she remembered.

She lay back down again and turned her back on him.

'Well I was warned about having a teenager in the house, but I didn't expect it would start so soon,' Dad said, his voice jokey, but with an edge of anxiety in it.

'It's no worse than *I* can expect from now on,' Sapphie said.

She felt Dad's arms round her.

'Get off!' she said through clenched teeth.

Dad got up. She heard the bedroom door shut.

Sapphie sat up.

When she had unwrapped the tiny package she closed her hand round the chunky gold locket. Her shoulders began to heave.

The door opened. Her mother came in and rushed up to her. 'What is it Sapphie? What on earth's the matter? Dad says you're in a terrible mood. Is it something we've done?'

'It's more something you're going to do,' Sapphie said, stifling a sob.

Her mother looked guilty. Then she leaned over and put her arms round Sapphie. 'You heard us last night,' she said. 'I'm so sorry, darling.' She waited for Sapphie to look at her. Then she said quietly, 'We didn't mean you to find out like that.'

'It's true then? You're going to split up. Get – divorced?' There. She'd said the word. Sapphie's voice shook.

Her mother lowered her eyes. 'You know what it's been like lately, Sapphie. You must have guessed something like that was going to happen,' she said.

'No!' Sapphie said ferociously. 'No! Everyone quarrels, Mum. Becky says their whole family quarrels.'

'But not all the time,' Mum said with a sigh. 'It's no good, Sapphie. Enough's enough. Anyway. It's your birthday. Let's be happy today, eh?' She lifted Sapphie's chin up and smiled at her. 'And you're a teenager now,' she said.

'And you've spoiled it for me!' Sapphie wailed.

At school she pretended everything was all right. She didn't even tell Becky about the divorce.

Especially Becky.

How many times had Becky said how she wished she was an only one like Sapphie? Instead of one of three. 'You get all the attention in your house. All the fuss. All the treats. Spoilt rotten you are. And nobody to quarrel with you.'

Nobody to share your problems with either, Sapphie thought now. It was her birthday. A special birthday. And all she could do was worry and fret.

It didn't get any better as the day developed and her party got nearer. She'd been looking forward to it so much. Now she couldn't get her head round it.

When she got home from school, she changed into her designer jeans and T-shirt, then dabbled with some make-up like she often did. Then she deliberately plastered the make-up on till her eyes stood out and her lips glistened. Mum always warned her about being too obvious with make-up. 'Less is best,' she said when she encouraged Sapphie to experiment. Just let her criticise now!

When she went downstairs, Mum opened her mouth and shut it. Dad winced. 'Not wearing your locket?' was all he said though.

Sapphie tossed her head. 'It would look stupid with this gear,' she said, and was glad when she saw the hurt on his face.

When they got to the bowling alley everyone stared at Sapphie. Was the make-up that bad she wondered? But didn't care.

And she couldn't be bothered either. She sent each bowl hurtling down, crashing inevitably down the side and scoring nothing.

'Better luck next time Sapphie,' Mum said.

But it didn't matter.

She didn't respond when her friends knocked seven, eight, nine pins down. Nor when another scored a strike. 'That's just a fluke,' she said, hard-eyed and tight-lipped. While the others leapt up and waved their arms around as if it was a miracle.

'You're in a funny mood,' Becky said. 'It's your birthday. Cheer up!'

'You're supposed to be moody when you're a teenager,' Sapphie said, trying to make a joke of it. Only she wasn't laughing. Then she saw Becky's face and relented. 'I'll tell you about it later,' she whispered, suddenly needing to tell her best friend after all. But having to wait now till the party was over.

The rest of the party didn't go any better. Today, nothing could lift Sapphie's mood.

She was a bad loser at the ten pins.

She wasn't grateful for any of her presents.

She didn't want to go to the Mexican, her favourite place to eat, and when they got there, criticised everything about it.

She was angry with her parents and angry with herself and relieved when it was over.

She supposed this feeling eating away inside her was what everyone meant by teenage *angst*. A strange word, she'd thought. Up till now. But now she knew exactly what it meant. And now it seemed just the right word. It meant how it sounded. Painful.

When it was all over and her friends had all gone except Becky, the mood that had been threatening her all day totally engulfed Sapphie.

She knew her friends had been disappointed with her at the party. She knew her parents were disappointed with her too. Well she was much more disappointed with them. If they'd only kept quiet for just one more day, at least she could have enjoyed her birthday. The lousy party was their fault. Not hers. Her behaviour was their fault. Not hers.

To round off the day, Becky came home with her. 'What's the matter, then?' she said when at last they were alone in Sapphie's bedroom.

'It's my parents, Becky.' She could hardly say it. 'They're going to get – divorced.' Her mouth quivered. 'Last night Mum said that it was all *over*. Meaning my family! She said about wanting a clean break. How could they, Becky?' she ended up. 'How *could* they?'

'I know they haven't been getting on recently, Saph, but your parents always seemed so right for each other,' Becky said. 'I thought they'd sort it out. I didn't think they'd ever split up.'

'I still can't believe it,' Sapphie said. 'Except my mum said it was true when I asked her straight out this morning.'

'You poor thing!' Becky said. 'And on your birthday.'

Now she'd got it, Sapphie wasn't sure she liked Becky's sympathy all that much. It felt wrong somehow. 'My parents *used* to get on,' she said. 'But not any more. That's the trouble. Every time they open their mouths now, it's to snipe at each other. I just never imagined—' she couldn't finish. Tried again. '—All those other kids it's happened to,' she said, 'and I've never given it a thought. Never felt the least bit

sorry for them. I feel sorry for myself now though.'
She paused. Gulped. 'What happens when people get
divorced, Becky?'

'Perhaps they won't,' Becky said. 'Everybody
quarrels. All the time. Perhaps they'll sort it out.
You'll see.'

Sapphie nodded thoughtfully. 'Perhaps I can make
sure they won't...' she said, beginning to feel more
positive than she'd felt all day. 'What if I were to get
into trouble at school, Becky? Then, they'd see what it
was doing to me. They'd blame themselves! And then
they'd have second thoughts, wouldn't they?' Her eyes
narrowed. 'I've got to stop them.' She bit her bottom
lip. 'So! How can I get into trouble, Becky? What can
I do?'

'I'm not sure that's the answer, Saph,' Becky said.

'Well, I've got to do something! Can't you see that,
Becky?'

Becky frowned. 'I suppose so...' she said reluctantly.

Both of their brows came together and they were
silent for a while.

Thoughts of pranks that kids got up to at school in
books flooded Sapphie's brain. But none of them
seemed in the least appropriate to her.

Then Sapphie had an idea. 'What about what I
don't do?' she said at last. 'How about if I suddenly

didn't do any more homework? The teachers would go bananas wouldn't they? And my parents would be bound to get to know about it. That should get them thinking, shouldn't it?'

She smiled for the first time that day.

Chapter Three

Sapphie didn't actually mind homework. She loved books and it was no hardship for her to get her schoolbooks out after school and get on with whatever was set. She took great pride in it.

But she stuck to the plan and stopped doing it.

The first day she brought no homework books home with her, it felt weird. And the next day when she handed nothing in, it felt even weirder. She felt lost. After a few days she felt really bad about it.

The results were mixed. Some teachers hardly seemed to notice. Others reminded her gently to make sure she did it promptly next time. And one or two told her off. As this was what she wanted she shouldn't have been so upset. But she was. Sapphie wasn't used to being told off. She wasn't used to being in trouble with teachers. And it made her feel bad about herself. But the idea was to get into trouble, wasn't it? So actually the teachers who told her off were the ones she should be grateful to, she told herself.

At home, homework had always been top of the agenda for support from her parents: 'Let's have a look at what you're doing, Sapphie,'; 'You are clever, Sapphie,'; 'I couldn't do that,' were some of the things they said to her every night.

When it stopped, at first they tried not to notice. Then they seemed puzzled.

'No homework again?' Mum said with a frown after a few days.

'I'll have to go down that school and sort them out,' Dad eventually said after another few days.

Good. Wasn't that exactly what Sapphie wanted? She kept to the plan doggedly. Even though one or two of her teachers were getting really nasty about it now.

'It's going to be all right you know,' Mum said. Broaching the unbroachable as she and Sapphie cleared up after a meal a few days later.

Was it working then? Sapphie thought. Was Mum putting two and two together because of the homework thing? Was she blaming herself? Would she change her mind?

'What does Kate think about what you're doing?' Sapphie suddenly asked.

'Kate?' Mum looked unsettled. 'Why do you want to know what she thinks?'

'Well, Kate's your friend. And mine.' Sapphie frowned. 'Does that mean she's not Dad's friend anymore? Is that how it's going to work, Mum?'

That stopped Mum in her tracks. 'Don't be silly, darling. Nobody stops being friends.'

'Only you two! The two most important people in my life,' Sapphie said.

Mum looked crestfallen. 'We'll sort it out, darling. I promise,' she said.

Sapphie drew in her breath. Did that mean what she hoped it might mean?

Later that evening, Dad looked up from his computer and noticed how miserable Sapphie was looking. He came over and put his arm round her and she cuddled up to him.

'You work too hard, Dad,' she said.

He grinned at her. Dad had a cheeky grin. It made him look like a boy.

'It keeps us in the way we're accustomed to, pet,' he said. Then his smile disappeared and he looked serious. 'It is going to be all right, you know, Sapphie,' he said. The exact same words as Mum. At least they agreed on something.

'And if it's going to be so *all right* then, why all the drama?' Sapphie said.

'What drama?' he said, looking surprised.

'It's all drama,' Sapphie retorted. 'Everything's a drama at the moment, Dad. You can't call our family breaking up *all right*!' Her voice was a squeak.

Suddenly Dad looked as miserable as her. 'Well it's bound to be – upsetting,' he said. 'Any upset is – upsetting.'

Dad was never one with words, Sapphie reflected. She put her hand in his. 'Perhaps if you and Mum spent more time together. Less time working?' she said.

'Oh, Sapphie,' Dad said. 'I wish it was that easy.'

'You mean it's more than that?' Sapphie said. Trying really hard to understand. 'It's Max, isn't it Dad?' Her voice broke. 'Does Mum like him more than she likes you? I want to know what's going to happen, Dad. What's going to happen to you. And Mum. And me. I don't want us to split up. We belong together.'

Dad squeezed her hand. But, 'Don't worry, pet,' was the best he could come up with.

How could he say that? Sapphie felt like – like – hitting him. Instead, she flounced up off the sofa and stalked upstairs.

When she was in bed, Mum came in to say good night. 'You see, Dad and me, we don't talk properly anymore,' she said. Sitting on the bed.

But Sapphie wasn't having any of that. 'There's an easy answer to that!' she snapped. Sitting up and facing Mum.

'No. It's not easy,' Mum said. 'It's very hard. When we do talk, we end up quarrelling. That's why things are so bad between us.'

But it sounded like a lot of excuses to Sapphie. 'You always tell me that if we talk about a problem we can

sort it out. Whatever the problem. So you can sort this out Mum, can't you?' she said desperately. Then she grabbed Mum. 'Please!' she begged.

Dad came in.

Mum moved up and made room for him on the bed. How they used to.

Then they both had a go at her. Together.

Oh well, Sapphie thought, it makes a change them being together on something.

'You know we both love you, don't you?' Mum said in a determined voice.

'Very much,' Dad said with a firm nod of the head.

Sapphie looked from one of them to the other. If it wasn't so sad it would be funny.

'That will never change,' Mum said.

'Never,' Dad echoed.

It sounded like they'd rehearsed it.

And Sapphie said so.

They both bristled.

'It's the truth,' Mum said, her voice rising.

'The absolute!' Dad said, his eyes wide.

'Well, how come *that* will never change when everything else will?' Sapphie yelled. And flung herself down on the bed and turned her back on them.

They left her room like two naughty children.

The next day they pulled out all the stops and took her out to supper at the Mexican. It was still her favourite place to eat, despite the fiasco at her birthday party.

They were still acting the normal family bit when Mum dropped the bombshell. 'Whichever one of us leaves—' she started to say '—Dad or me—'

Sapphie didn't hear the rest. Just their voices droning on. Then she saw their faces. Expectant. Waiting.

'Did you hear what we said, darling?' Mum said.

Sapphie shook her head. 'No!' she said emphatically. Meaning neither of them must leave, not that she hadn't heard what they'd said. It didn't matter what else they'd said.

'We said – it's up to you, darling.' Mum was struggling. Her face was red. She looked very uncomfortable. It was most unlike her. 'We're not going to influence you one way or the other,' she said. 'We won't put any pressure on you. You stay with which one of us you want to. And whichever one you – live with – and wherever…' her voice faltered, '…the other one will still be there for you,' she finished lamely.

So there it was. They were asking her to choose. And it sounded every bit as horrific as Sapphie'd thought it would.

She leapt up, dragging her cutlery off the table. It clanged on to the tiled floor. 'How could you?' she yelled.

For a moment, everything in the restaurant went quiet except the ringing of the cutlery on the floor. Her parents got up. The waiter came over to the table.

'Can I have the bill please?' Dad said.

Her parents didn't know what to say to her on the way home. They seemed as distressed as she was. Nobody spoke.

When they arrived home, Sapphie rushed straight up to her bedroom and curled up tight in bed. Now she could have a good cry.

Chapter Four

'I've got to choose, Becky,' she said. Walking round the playground at break the next day.

Becky didn't know what to say.

Sapphie stopped. Stood still. Stared at Becky. 'They say it's up to me,' she said miserably. 'But how can I choose? If I stay with Mum, I won't be with Dad. And if I stay with Dad, I won't be with Mum. I can't bear it, Becky.' Her voice was wretched.

Becky looped her arm through Sapphie's and they walked on arm in arm. 'But you'll visit the other one,' she said, her voice coaxing. 'And they'll both spoil you rotten.'

'They spoil me rotten anyway. You know that. That'll be nothing new.'

'Presents. Places to go,' Becky said, doing her best to be a comfort. 'Divorced kids say it's a good deal.'

'I get presents already,' Sapphie said. Refusing to be comforted. 'They take me places now.' Her shoulders slumped. 'You know I might have to move? I might even have to change schools. All I want is for things to stay as they are,' she said.

Later, she went home from school with Becky.

Becky's mother worked part-time but was always home for Becky when she got home from school. And her two brothers. And there was a pet rabbit. A cat. And a gerbil. At Becky's house there was always somebody around. Something happening. A discussion here. A discussion there. A row here. A row there. Their mum acting as referee. And a cuddle for everyone. Including Sapphie.

Usually Sapphie loved being here. Today, though, she felt miserable. And it felt like she hated them all. Even Becky. Because it suddenly seemed to her that Becky, who'd always envied *her*, had everything that Sapphie now wanted. Mum. Dad. Brothers. Pets. Happy families!

Sapphie found herself clenching her hands till her nails bit into them.

In the seclusion of her bedroom that night, Sapphie reasoned that if she got into enough trouble at school, often enough, her parents would relent. The homework thing was fizzling out. She couldn't keep it up. At least while her head was buried in a book she could forget about her worries. She had to come up with something else. Then her parents would see that they were making things impossible for her. Then, for her sake, they'd change their minds. After all, they were her parents. And they loved her. They were always telling her that. And she was a teenager now, when things were supposed to be difficult. And when parents were supposed to be there for her.

But as someone who found it natural to behave well, and who was always anxious to please, Sapphie was surprised how difficult it was to come up with something that would land her in real trouble...

Then, when she saw Janice Long in the playground the next day, she had an idea.

Janice was looking her usual self. Hair matted. Eyes lined despite frequent warnings from their form teacher. Her regulation skirt shorter than anyone else's. The shirt grubbier.

Janice was always the one in trouble in their class. Trouble seemed to follow her around. It came naturally to her. It was second nature.

What if Sapphie was to tag along with her? Wouldn't the trouble rub off on her?

Back in class, Sapphie manoeuvred her way next to Janice. Becky sent her a strange look and kept her distance. But Sapphie knew exactly what she was doing.

It wasn't long before Janice started talking to Sapphie. The teacher sent warning glances their way more than once but Janice continued talking. And Sapphie made herself chat back.

'Janice Long! Sapphie Squires!' the now irate teacher finally stopped the lesson. 'Is there something so urgent you have to say to each other that it can't wait till break? Is it perhaps something we should all share?'

The class giggled.

Becky frowned.

Sapphie squirmed.

But Janice just stared at the teacher. 'No, sir, it's nothing important,' she said and grinned at Sapphie.

At the next break, when Sapphie attached herself to Janice again, Janice seemed quite pleased. 'Is something up with you today, Sapphie Squires?' she said.

'Something. Everything,' Sapphie said.

Janice smirked.

'It's parent trouble,' Sapphie said confidentially. Appealing to Janice's better nature. If she had one.

Janice leaned over Sapphie, a satisfied look in her eyes. 'Join the club.'

'They're getting divorced,' Sapphie said.

'Is that all?' Janice said and seemed to lose interest in Sapphie.

But Sapphie followed her. 'Are your parents divorced then, Janice?' she said.

'Never married. My mum's always been on her own. Well. Most of the time anyway. I prefer it that way. There's a bloke on the scene at the moment though. And I don't like it. It always means trouble.'

For the rest of that break, Sapphie tagged on with Janice and her mates.

And at dinner break.

And in class she stuck to her like a leech. By the end of the day Sapphie had drawn more attention to herself for the wrong reasons, than she had at any other time since she'd been at the school.

After school she caught up with Becky queuing for the school bus and tried to explain to her. But Becky thought going round with Janice was going too far. And said so. 'I'm not having anything to do with Janice Long,' she said.

Sapphie sighed. Why was life so complicated now?

With Mum away, Sapphie went round Kate's for supper.

Kate had never been married. She worked in fashion, and flitted from one glamorous assignment to another.

'Why have you never married, Kate?' Sapphie asked her as they sat at the kitchen table over their avocado and crispy bacon salad. Kate, with her short red hair and her clashing red lipstick, was the picture of assurance.

'Too much to do. Too many places to be. Too many people to accommodate,' Kate said.

Which surprised Sapphie. 'You don't think you're missing out then?' she said.

Kate laughed. 'The only thing possibly missing in my life is a delightful daughter like you,' she said. 'I've never wanted to be with one person for long enough to be married.' Then she looked serious. 'Is this to do with what's happening at home?' she said, holding Sapphie's sad brown eyes.

Sapphie's face crumpled. She nodded. 'Is that what's gone wrong with Mum and Dad?' she said. 'Not wanting to be with one person any more? Especially me?'

Kate leaned over the table and put a hand over Sapphie's. 'No. No. No,' she said. 'You're the best thing that happened to them and they know it. They adore you. You know that.'

'So why are they doing the one thing I don't want them to, then?' Sapphie said. 'Why are they doing the one thing that will make me the most saddest miserable-est daughter ever anywhere?'

Kate gave a wry smile. 'It's nothing to do with you, Sapphie. It's to do with the two of them. They're not getting on. And they can't stay together just because you want them to. That wouldn't be right would it?'

'Why not?' Sapphie said. Because that was exactly what she wanted them to do.

Kate came round the table and put an arm round her shoulders. 'You love them both don't you, Sapphie?' she said.

'Course I do. That's why I want to live with them both,' Sapphie said.

'But you don't want them to be miserable for ever more, do you?' Kate said.

Sapphie swallowed hard. 'You think they're miserable living with me?'

'They're miserable living *together*, Sapphie. Believe me, it's nothing to do with you. But you don't want your parents to be permanently miserable, do you?'

'I want us all to be happy like we used to be,' Sapphie said.

'I suppose they would like that too,' Kate said. 'But it's just not possible any more. They didn't plan things to happen like this.' She stared at Sapphie. 'It'll be all right,' she said. 'You'll see.'

'You're at it now, Kate. *They* keep telling me that. Why can't you all see that it's never going to be all right again?'

Chapter Five

At school, Sapphie started to spend more and more time with Janice. And Becky looked more and more down in the mouth about it every day. 'I'm fed up with it, Sapphie,' she eventually said one morning as they walked into school together. 'You prefer to be friends with her now, don't you?' she said, her voice rising.

Sapphie felt bad about it and hung her head. But at the moment being with Becky reminded her of the time when everything was all right. While being with Janice reminded her that everything wasn't all right, *and* that she was trying to do something about it.

'I never thought you'd prefer her to me, Sapphie,' Becky persisted angrily.

'It's not as easy as that—' Sapphie tried to explain. But Becky interrupted her. '—yes it is! You sit next to her in class. You go around with her at breaktime. You obviously like her more than me. Well I wish you well of her. You're welcome to her!'

She stormed off.

Sapphie wished things could be different, but had to stick to her plan for the time being.

Janice seemed flattered by Sapphie's attention. When she noticed Becky moping round the classroom she had a gloating look on her face. And when she saw the looks of disapproval on their teachers' faces, she grinned. Because as Sapphie spent more time with Janice, she found herself in all sorts of trouble. The talking in class became a habit and she soon found herself in detention for the first time in her life. She didn't like it. But reasoned that things were going how she wanted them to. Wasn't this what she was after, she excused herself? Wasn't this what she'd hoped for? Wasn't it proving quite easy to get into trouble after all?

It was one morning when Sapphie and Janice were in the surge of kids going up the corridor to the next lesson, that Janice suggested they bunk off.

But this scared Sapphie. She had never missed a lesson in her life.

Janice had already turned round against the tide of kids, though.

'There are much better things to do than go to maths. Are you coming with me?' she called as she pushed her way back down the corridor.

Sapphie guessed she should be flattered that Janice had asked her rather than one of her other mates. So she turned and elbowed her way back down the corridor after her. Worrying, at the same time, about whether the maths teacher would notice she wasn't there. And what would he say if he did notice? Would the other kids split on them? And what would Becky think? What would happen if they got caught out?

Janice led Sapphie outside, down to the school field.

'What shall we do now?' Sapphie asked anxiously.

'Doesn't really matter, does it? As long as it's not maths,' Janice said with a giggle. 'Let's go for a walk.'

'What if someone sees us?' Sapphie said. There had to be a good reason for any student being out in the grounds in lesson time.

'So they see us,' Janice said. Unconcerned. Sapphie wondered how long it took to be like Janice. Her own heart was thumping madly.

'You are a misery, Sapphie Squires. I wish I'd asked someone else to come with me now,' Janice said.

'No. No. I'm enjoying myself,' Sapphie lied. 'It's just I've never done this before.'

Janice laughed. 'Little Miss Innocent. Let's go the

whole hog, then. Let's get out of school.'

But there had to be a very good reason for being out of school in school time! As Sapphie followed Janice, her hands felt sweaty.

They went out the back field way, which they weren't supposed to do either. And as they wandered round the streets, Sapphie found herself stooping as if she was trying to make herself invisible.

When they came to a small parade of shops Janice said, 'Got any money on you?'

Sapphie felt in her pockets and pulled out some coins. 'That's enough,' Janice said.

They went in a shop and bought two cans of coke and some sweets, then made their way to the park nearby.

They sat on the swings slurping their coke and eating sweets. 'This is better than maths, isn't it, Saph?' Janice said.

Sapphie wasn't exactly enjoying herself, but she began to relax. No one else was around.

Then a middle-aged woman came into the park walking a dog. She frowned at them disapprovingly. 'Why aren't you in school?' she said and Sapphie looked guilty.

But Janice gave her the eye. 'Why don't you mind your own business?' she said.

Sapphie kept her head down in embarrassment.

The woman walked on, shaking her head.

'Nosy cow!' Janice said. She called after her, 'And make sure you clean up after your dog.'

Sapphie looked at her watch. 'It's nearly lunch time,' she said anxiously.

Janice laughed. 'Back we go then,' she said. 'But we'll do this again, eh?'

Back at school, Becky was one of the first people Sapphie saw in the dining room. 'Where were you in maths?' she said accusingly.

Sapphie didn't reply.

'Skiving off with Janice Long,' Stephie Peters said, standing nearby.

'Mind your own,' Sapphie said. Sounding like Janice.

Stephie grabbed Becky's arm and the two of them found a table and sat down together. For the rest of the day Stephie Peters went around with Becky.

The next time Janice suggested to Sapphie that they bunk off, she suggested they took the whole day. At that Sapphie was seriously afraid. But she didn't want Janice knowing that. 'Where shall we go? What'll we do?' she said.

'We'll go into town. Do the shopping precinct,' Janice said. 'It'll be cool.'

So the next day, instead of getting on the school bus, Sapphie caught a bus to town and met Janice at the shopping precinct.

'How much have you got then?' Janice said.

She was impressed as Sapphie pulled out some banknotes.

They had coffee in a coffee bar, spooning the delicious froth of a cappuccino into their mouths and laughing at the chocolate moustaches they acquired.

This wasn't too bad, Sapphie thought.

They experimented at all the make-up counters, trying out the products till the assistants sent them packing. Then Sapphie bought them both a lip gloss just to show the assistants that they had money to spend if they wanted to.

But no matter how hard she tried, Sapphie wasn't really enjoying herself. And after they'd treated themselves to a baguette at a food bar at lunch time, she wished they could go back to school. She was getting more and more twitchy as the day wore on.

Janice, however, was obviously enjoying herself. After they'd eaten, she led Sapphie into clothes store after clothes store, rifling through racks of clothes. Janice drooled over the clothes like a deprived child in a sweet shop.

At last it was nearly home time.

'We'd better be making tracks,' Janice said. And Sapphie sighed with relief. When they'd caught a bus home, Janice grinned. 'It's been a brilliant day,' she said, sounding more enthusiastic than Sapphie had ever heard her. 'We must do it again soon.'

When she got home, Sapphie wondered if she'd been missed at school. Part of her wanted to be found out. Wasn't the idea to get into as much trouble as possible after all? But there was a big part of her that still didn't want to be found out…

The next day, Mr Marr, her form teacher, asked Sapphie if she was ill yesterday. He reminded her about sick notes. And left it at that. She didn't know whether to be pleased or not.

He gave Janice a harder time, though, as she was a more persistent absentee. But Janice just shrugged it off.

Becky shook her head at Sapphie. 'I never thought you'd do such a thing,' she said, looking shocked.

Becky was now spending more and more time with Stephie Peters.

Sapphie was jealous. But there wasn't much she could do about it...

Chapter Six

It wasn't long before Janice suggested they bunk off again. Sapphie was less afraid this time. Knowing what to expect. But still feeling twitchy about it.

They went to another precinct this time. 'No point in covering the same ground,' Janice said.

They followed the same routine. Coffee. The make-up counters. Lunch. The clothes shops. Till Janice spotted something she badly wanted.

'Look at this T-shirt, Saph,' she said, pulling out a T-shirt covered in graffiti. 'This is me. I want it.'

'How much is it?' Sapphie said. She hadn't got much money left.

'Don't worry, Saph,' Janice said. And bundled the T-shirt into her bag.

Sapphie was horrified, but Janice giggled. 'Don't worry,' she said. 'It's not tagged.'

She rushed out of the shop, Sapphie in tow.

The next thing Sapphie knew someone was behind them. 'Can I have a look in your bag, miss,' he said, and took Janice's bag from her.

Janice didn't have time to object.

Sapphie froze.

The man found the T-shirt screwed up. 'Have you got a receipt for this item, miss?' he said. Knowing she hadn't. Janice said she'd dropped it, but it was obvious she was lying. 'Can you come back into the shop, miss?' he said.

Sapphie looked on.

'And you, miss,' the man said.

Sapphie was mortified.

They were taken through the shop into an office at the back, where they were met by the manager of the shop.

He immediately started making phone calls.

One to school.

Another to their parents. Only he wouldn't be able to get hold of her parents, Sapphie thought. Mum being away. And Dad on some computer course somewhere. But he rang Kate anyway, Kate's being the alternative contact number. Sapphie gulped. What would Kate think? she wondered.

Then the manager rang the police. 'The usual,' he said. His voice weary. 'Can you send someone down?'

Sapphie gulped again. She couldn't believe this was happening to her. She just wanted to disappear. Longed, now, for things to be back to normal. If there was any such thing as normal. She wished desperately that she was back at school sitting next to Becky. Becky was right. Being Janice's friend was turning out to be just too risky. She wasn't cut out for being a criminal. She didn't even want to be labelled a nuisance. Not really.

If only her parents were staying together then none of this would be happening.

But when she looked at the stern face of the manager and he glared reproachfully back at her, she realised it was all a bit late for wishing.

There was a wait now while the manager busied himself with papers on his desk.

Would they be arrested when the police came, Sapphie wondered? What would happen to them then? What would they say at school? What would Kate say? Her parents? She hadn't dreamed things would come to this.

Janice drummed her fingers on her knee and stared around defiantly.

The door opened and someone led in Miss
Marriott. Miss Marriott was the teacher who dealt
with all the problem kids at school. She shook the
shop manager's hand with a sigh. She'd obviously
done this before. 'I'm very sorry,' she said and stared
at the two girls. Then shook her head at Sapphie.
'You're the last student I expected to see here,' she
said.

'What about me, miss?' Janice said and sniggered.

'You'd better watch what you say,' the shop
manager said. 'You're in deep trouble, my girl.'

Miss Marriott sent a penetrating stare Janice's way and Janice dropped her eyes. 'I didn't mean to do it, miss,' she mumbled.

Miss Marriott sat down, and the waiting started again.

There was a knock on the door and this time a policeman put his head round it. He came in, closely followed by a policewoman.

There was a whispered conversation with the manager then they sat down too.

More waiting.

The policeman and woman stared at the girls.

Miss Marriott stared at the girls.

The manager stared at them.

Sapphie looked down at the floor.

Janice stared back.

There was another knock on the door and this time it was Janice's mother who was led in. She clipped Janice round the ear. Janice gave a yelp. 'You might do that, my girl!' her mother said.

'That's enough,' the policeman said to her. Then he looked at Janice. 'You've got yourself into this mess. Only got yourself to blame,' he added.

'I didn't mean to do it,' Janice mumbled. 'It was a spur of the moment thing.'

'Hmm!' the manager grunted. 'They all say that,' he said. He put his elbows onto the desk. Rested his chin on his fists. Stared at them again.

Then Kate appeared. When she gave Sapphie a reassuring little look, Sapphie felt like crying. She wished she could curl up into a ball on the floor and disappear.

That was everyone.

The policeman stood up. 'Right. I could start talking

about arrests now—' he said. Paused.

Janice gulped.

Sapphie began to cry.

'But—' the policeman added. Keeping them in suspense.

'—But if it's a first offence it shouldn't come to that,' the policewoman finished for him more kindly.

'Have you ever done this sort of thing before?' the manager asked them.

'No,' Janice said.

Sapphie shook her head vehemently.

'I can assure you that they've never been in this sort of trouble before,' Miss Marriott said. 'And we'll do our best to make sure they don't do it again.' She sent a stony stare the girls' way.

'Right. As it is a first offence, then, ' the manager said, 'I won't prosecute. You're getting a caution only. But we have your names,' he added. 'All the shops have a list of persistent offenders, you know. And you're both on it now. So be warned.' He leaned over to Miss Marriott. 'I hope you can get through to them, Miss Marriott.'

Sapphie could swear Janice nearly laughed.

Miss Marriott sent her a withering stare. 'Count yourself lucky, Janice,' she said. 'And don't think we'll be so lenient at school.'

'Nor at home!' Janice's mother said.

Janice looked down and jiggled her foot.

'Sorry, Miss Marriott,' Sapphie said. 'Very sorry, sir,' she said to the manager. She attempted a smile at Kate.

Miss Marriott stared at Janice. 'So-rry,' Janice said in a singsong voice.

Chapter Seven

On the way back to school Sapphie had time to think. Truanting. Shoplifting. Nearly being arrested. Kate knew all about it now. Soon, her parents would too. And they would be aghast. Which was just what she'd wanted, wasn't it? They were bound to rethink now, weren't they?

But then she remembered what Kate'd said about them not getting on. Not wanting them to be miserable. And she gave a long wavering sigh. She wasn't sure about anything anymore.

Back at school the class soon got to know about what had happened. Apart from Janice's mates, they all gave Janice and Sapphie the cold shoulder. Including Becky. Sapphie wasn't used to this and hated it.

Miss Marriott interviewed the girls individually.

'I've managed to get hold of your father, Sapphie. And he's told me that you're going through a difficult time at home. So I'm going to make allowances for that,' she said.

Sapphie was aghast that the school knew their business.

'But there's a lot more going on than this escapade today. I gather that none of your teachers are happy about your progress at the moment, Sapphie. And it needs discussing with both your parents. When they're available,' she added, with a hint of implied criticism.

Sapphie should be glad her parents were going to be involved at last. Wasn't this what she'd been trying to do from the beginning? But nevertheless, she dreaded seeing the disappointment on their faces.

It was a week before the meeting could be arranged.

Then Sapphie found herself at school in the small studio, sitting with Miss Marriott and Mr Marr, waiting for her parents to arrive. And as she waited, she realised that it was the first time in her life she had dreaded them coming up to school about anything. And she didn't like the feeling.

They were sitting in comfortable armchairs grouped casually in a circle.

Non-threatening, if a little obvious, Sapphie thought.

At last the knock came on the door.

Miss Marriott got up and opened the door. Greeted her parents, who smiled sheepishly at Sapphie. They both looked nervous. Not their usual style.

'Would you like a cup of coffee. Or tea?' Mr Marr said, going over to the machines.

'Coffee will be fine,' her mother said.

And her father.

They all sat down as drinks were poured and handed round.

Sapphie fidgeted on her chair.

Mr Marr picked up a file and opened it. 'Now,' he said, looking round the group. 'Sapphie was always one of our best students—' past tense, Sapphie noted, '—not only was she conscientious, but she always seemed to enjoy her work. And she's always taken a full part in the social life of the school. Got on well with her peers. A model student in fact.'

'Till recently,' Miss Marriott said.

It was obviously going to be a two-pronged attack.

'Now. You told me that there are marital problems, Mr Squires,' Mr Marr said matter-of-factly.

Her dad nodded his head and coughed nervously.

Sapphie flinched.

Mum tried to engage Sapphie's attention, but Sapphie refused to look at her.

'So we fully appreciate that it's a bad time for all of you,' Mr Marr continued. 'But we can't ignore the effect it's having on Sapphie.'

Brilliant! Sapphie thought. That was just what she was after.

'Her recent work has been disappointing.' Mr Marr frowned at Sapphie. 'And now this – incident.'

'We need to take stock,' Miss Marriott said.

Both her parents looked more than uncomfortable now.

'We'll do anything it takes,' her father said.

'Yes,' her mother agreed.

Except the one thing that *would* sort it, Sapphie thought. She looked at her parents, suddenly feeling defiant.

'How can we help?' her mother said in a small voice. Now it was her avoiding Sapphie's eyes.

'We don't usually try to influence friendship groupings,' Mr Marr said. 'It's best to let these things take their natural course. Trying to influence such things often has the opposite effect anyway,' he said. 'But Sapphie's choice of friends lately has been – to say the least – misguided.' Careful to name no names, Sapphie noted. He stared at Sapphie. 'We want you to take note of what's being said, Sapphie. We've been looking closely into your behaviour recently and discover that you've missed lessons before. I'm disappointed in you, Sapphie.' He paused. Sapphie felt dreadful. 'But this shoplifting incident is much more serious,' he said. 'We've established that you weren't involved in the actual act, but you were there when you should have been at school.' There was a longer pause, while everyone considered what he was saying. 'From now on, we'll be watching you very carefully, Sapphie,' he finally said.

Her parents sighed deeply.

'We had no idea,' her mother said.

Her father shook his head.

'We want to get Sapphie back on course, Mr and Mrs Squires,' Mr Marr said. 'We want you enthusiastic about school again, Sapphie,' he said directly to Sapphie. 'About life in general,' he added.

'We'll do what we can to encourage her,' her father said.

'And to reassure her,' her mother added.

Sapphie looked at her parents. It was up to them now.

Miss Marriott looked at her parents. 'There's family counselling available if you want it,' she said quietly, as if she was treading carefully.

'In the meantime,' Mr Marr said, 'let's see how things go now we've had this little chat. And remember, Sapphie, we'll be keeping a close eye on things from now on.' He looked at her parents. 'But if anything like this incident happens again, it could be much more serious next time.' He paused. Letting them take in the implications of what he'd said. 'In the meantime, Mr and Mrs Squires, we'll be filling in a weekly report card for Sapphie. And your comments will be most welcome.' He looked at Sapphie. 'You and Becky,' he suddenly said. 'What happened there, Sapphie? You were such good friends. And good for each other.'

Sapphie's face fell. The fact was that she'd ignored Becky and Becky was now ignoring her. And now, everywhere that Becky went, Stephie Peters went with her.

She mumbled something about Stephie Peters being Becky's friend now.

Mr Marr got up. Proffered a hand to her parents in turn. 'We'll be grateful for your on-going co-operation from now on, Mr and Mrs Squires,' he said.

'Yes. Of course. Thank you,' her parents said together.

When she saw Janice, Janice was flippant about her interview. 'Talk about the gestapo. They put the fear of God into me,' she said and laughed.

At home, later, her parents said, 'It's that Janice.'

'Too streetwise for you, Sapphie.'

Which made Sapphie mad. Even though she knew it was true.

'We know what's going on,' Mum said. 'You're disorientated by what's happening here at home.'

'And what's that supposed to mean?' Sapphie said.

'It's like they said. Because you're – we're unsettled,' Mum said. Dad looked on, decidedly put out.

'You didn't mean to go off the rails.'

'It's just a temporary glitch. You wait—'

Here it comes again, Sapphie thought.

'—we know things are difficult for all of us just now, Sapphie. But they'll settle down again. You'll see. Everything will be all right soon.'

Sapphie was rigid with resentment. 'Don't be so stupid!' she yelled. 'As far as I'm concerned, nothing is ever going to be all right again. Can't you see that?'

Then it suddenly came to her. *The only thing possibly missing in my life is a delightful daughter like you*, Kate'd said.

Well. That could be arranged. 'And I don't want to live with either of you,' she yelled at her parents. 'I want to live with Kate!'

Chapter Eight

The next day, Sapphie rang Kate and asked when she could go round.

Kate said she was working from home that day and Sapphie could go round later.

'And how are things now?' she asked Sapphie when Sapphie arrived.

'It depends what things you mean, Kate. I'm on report at school. Like some naughty little girl. And at home, you probably know more of what's going on than me. They just keep telling me everything's going to be all right.'

Kate plumped the cushions up in her large comfortable sofa and sat Sapphie down. Then she sat down next to her and tucked her feet under her. Sapphie tucked her feet under her too so they were sitting sideways looking at each other.

'Kate,' Sapphie said, a nervous tone in her voice.

Kate smiled encouragingly.

'Do you remember what you said about the one thing missing from your life?'

Kate frowned. 'I thought I had it all, actually,' she said flippantly. 'What did I say, pet?'

Sapphie's eyes were like saucers. 'You said, "The only thing possibly missing in my life is a delightful daughter like you." That's what you said.' Sapphie quoted her word for word.

'Did I say that?'

'Are you saying it's not true, then?' Sapphie said, suddenly losing confidence.

Kate frowned. 'Of course it's true, pet. But where is this going? You're very serious.'

Sapphie grabbed Kate's hand. 'Yes I am serious, Kate. There's a lot of very serious things going on in my life at the moment,' she said dramatically. 'My parents have said I must choose between them. But you know I don't want to. I can't. How can I choose between them when I love them both equally?' She took a deep breath. 'So I've told them I want to live with you.'

Kate's eyes registered something. Sapphie wasn't sure what. There was an uneasy silence. 'Let's have a drink,' she said and got up. 'Coke or fruit juice?'

Sapphie got up and followed Kate into her small neat kitchen. 'Coke,' she said.

Kate got some ice out of the fridge. The three cubes clinked as she dropped them into each of two tall glasses. Then she sliced some lemon and put a slice in each glass. Lastly, she poured the foaming brown liquid over the ice and lemon and passed a glass to Sapphie.

'What do you say, Kate?' Sapphie asked, catching her breath anxiously. 'Can I come and live with you?'

'I'm very honoured—' Kate began.

Sapphie smiled.

'—but, '

Sapphie stopped drinking.

'You remember what else I said, Sapphie? About too much to do. Too many places to be. Too many people to accommodate.'

Kate took her drink through to the lounge and sat down again. Sapphie followed. Then she stared at Kate, willing her to look back at her. When she did, Sapphie stared urgently and intently into Kate's eyes. 'But you said that about me too, Kate,' she said. 'You did.' Her voice trailed off.

'But abandoning your parents. Think about it, Sapphie,' Kate said quietly.

'They're abandoning each other. And one of them will abandon me,' Sapphie said.

'No. Never. They wouldn't abandon you, Sapphie. You're top of both of their list of priorities.'

'But it doesn't feel like that,' Sapphie said. 'So living with you would be the best solution, Kate. And I want to.'

Kate grabbed Sapphie and hugged her tight. 'I'm very very honoured, pet,' she said again. 'And flattered.' She drew apart from Sapphie and looked at her. 'But going to live with your mother's best friend isn't going to solve anything really, is it?' she said gently.

Sapphie frowned. 'Why not?' she asked stubbornly.

Kate was quiet for a while. As if she was thinking hard. 'If I had a daughter, Sapphie, I would want her to be exactly like you.'

Sapphie frowned again. 'Even after what's happened recently?' she asked.

'Even after what's happened recently,' Kate said, grabbing Sapphie's hand tight. 'You've only been trying to grab your parents' attention.'

Sapphie gulped. She was so glad that Kate understood that. Then she found herself telling Kate all about Janice and how she'd wanted to get into trouble and how being friends with Janice had seemed like a good idea. And how Becky was upset. How everything was going wrong for her at the moment.

'Janice isn't right for you, my pet,' Kate said. 'I should try and make it up with Becky.'

'But it's not as easy as that, Kate. Becky has a new friend now. Stephie Peters. So that leaves me and Janice. And the longer it goes on, the harder it seems to be to change things back to how they were.' In a moment of insight, Sapphie saw that this was perhaps how it was with Mum and Dad.

'You must try and make it up with Becky,' Kate said insistently. 'And about your parents—'

Sapphie was listening intently.

'—they do love you. And they couldn't bear to lose you. You must hold on to that. Whatever happens between them is between them. It's nothing to do with you. That's the most important thing to remember. I love you too. But not as much as your parents do. That's not possible.'

She suddenly loosened up. 'And you'd hate living with me,' she said with a giggle. 'I'm much too selfish.'

But Sapphie shook her head. 'I don't think you're selfish at all,' she said.

Kate got up. 'But now, pet,' she said, 'I'm afraid I've got some work to do.'

That night Mum had a long chat with Kate on the phone.

Afterwards, she came up to Sapphie's room and sat on her bed.

'Kate said you told her you wanted to live with her,' she said.

'What did she say, Mum?'

'She said you didn't really,' Mum said.

Sapphie pulled a face.

'It's just you can't choose between us. You're torn.' Mum sighed. 'We know how difficult it is for you, darling. It's breaking our hearts to see you so unhappy. We're bending over backwards to try and make it as easy as possible for you, you know. Making things as normal as possible. Keeping things low key.'

She hugged Sapphie tight.

'Kate said perhaps that's the trouble,' Mum continued. Letting go of her. 'She said if we got on with things and got them sorted out, it would be easier for you to accept it in the long run.' She looked at Sapphie anxiously.

But Sapphie didn't want this conversation.

'It's not easy to get things sorted though, Sapphie,' Mum continued nervously. Opening up at last. 'There's so much to settle. We've both got good jobs. But it's not a bottomless pit. And it all takes time. But—' she gave a quick little smile '—I think it will turn out that I stay here. And you'll stay with me.

Won't you?' she said. Sounding as near to desperate as Sapphie had ever heard her.

The question hung in the air. But it was the question that Sapphie wasn't sure about and still couldn't face up to. She shook her head stubbornly. 'I'm not choosing between you and Dad,' she insisted. 'I can't. I'd still rather choose Kate.'

'Darling. Kate isn't an option,' Mum said. Pausing and swallowing hard. 'She doesn't know you like we do. She's not used to thirteen-year-olds. It's one thing to have you for the evening. Another to have you to live. It's just not possible.'

'Nobody cares!' Sapphie sobbed. 'Nobody cares about me and what I want.'

'Of course we care.' Her mum got hold of her and rocked her like when she was a baby. 'We care so much, Sapphie.'

Later, when she should have been sleeping, Sapphie's mind leapt from one thing to another. How she always used to get good marks at school. How she'd got commendations for being co-operative. Getting on with everybody. How she hadn't even had to work at these things. They'd just happened. And how, now, her books were plastered with the sort of comments she could never have envisaged a while back. *Too brief. Sloppy work. You're not trying, Sapphie.*

It was what she'd intended. And yet it made her feel sick. And, she thought, not for the first time, that the more things were going wrong for her, the harder it seemed to put them right.

Her heart now ached when she thought about Becky. But all she saw now was Becky wandering round the playground arm in arm with Stephie Peters. Or huddled in a corner with her. Just like she used to be with Sapphie.

While *she* had Janice. Even the teachers seemed to be accepting that she hung out with Janice now.

Sapphie was doing her best to give the impression that none of this bothered her. It was what she wanted. The trouble was, underneath it all, it did bother her. Very much. And it was hurting.

She never brought Janice home though. And she never went home with Janice. She never went home with anyone now. And no one came home with her. At home she was alone with her thoughts and her problems and her worries.

Like now. When she added insomnia to her list of woes.

Kate rang her the next day and said, 'I'm expecting you for tea, pet.'

Eagerly, Sapphie went round. Perhaps Kate had changed her mind.

The kitchen smelt of cooking. Kate had pulled out all the stops. She served up spaghetti with anchovies, chilli and gorgeous garlicky toasted breadcrumbs. They both cleaned their plates. Then Kate sat back and rubbed her stomach. 'That's better. You can always talk better on a full tum.'

'Have you changed your mind, Kate?' Sapphie got straight to the point.

Kate frowned. 'How do you mean, Sapphie?'

'About me living with you,' Sapphie didn't finish.

'Your mum did tell you didn't she, Sapphie? About her wanting you to live with *her*. Or your dad. They both want you. That's what matters, Sapphie.' Kate paused.

'But what about you?' Sapphie said in a small voice.

'Sapphie. I explained what a selfish creature I am. That's why I live on my own. I told you. You know how much I love you. But I'd make a lousy mother.'

'But—' Sapphie said.

Kate interrupted her. 'But nothing, Sapphie. I'd be the worst person in the world to live with. That's what I want you to know. As I said before, I'm honoured and flattered that you want to live with me. But there are two people desperate for you to live with one of them. That's what you need to know.' She got up. 'Now. Let's see if I can find some pudding for us.'

Over the next few days and nights Sapphie chose one parent then the other. Imagined what it would be like with one without the other. And vice versa.

It would be all right with Dad, she supposed. He'd let her have all her favourite meals. When she wanted. He'd let her have as much chocolate and ice cream as she wanted. When. He'd let her watch whatever TV she wanted. When. There'd be no set mealtimes or bedtimes. Dad didn't see the point in routines. He'd never had one, and didn't see why they were necessary. But that would get a bit boring after a while wouldn't it? She thought. And she'd get fat.

It would be different with Mum. Mum thrived on routines. She had routines for everything. In the morning it was shower, dress, make-up. Then face the world. Mum hated slouching round in the morning in a dressing gown. And she absolutely insisted on a healthy diet. But wouldn't that get boring too?

No. Sapphie definitely needed both her parents with both lifestyles combined. That's what made her life good. It wouldn't work one without the other.

The next time she brushed past her dad and he grinned at her, she couldn't imagine him not being around.

And the next time she waved Mum goodbye as she went off to work, she couldn't bear the thought of her not coming back.

It always ended up the same.

At school Sapphie mooched round corridors with Janice, often arriving late to classes. But not skipping them any more. After school, they mooched round the streets. Sitting on pavements talking about nothing. Hanging around kids' playgrounds sitting on the swings. Mooching round the shops. Though Sapphie refused to go in any shops with Janice. Janice called her chicken, but Sapphie was too scared about what'd happened last time.

She'd never bunked off school since that other time, either.

Till now.

Chapter Nine

It all started when Janice got talking about theme parks.

'I suppose you've been to Disneyland?' she said to Sapphie.

Sapphie had to admit she had.

'America or France?' Janice said.

'Both,' Sapphie said.

'I've never even been to Alton Towers,' Janice admitted. She looked really peeved.

'I haven't,' Sapphie said. Pleased.

Janice looked pleased too. 'Shall we go then?' she said.

Sapphie was dubious.

'We could hitch,' Janice said.

Sapphie realised that Janice meant just the two of them.

'Right. Right,' she said apprehensively. But inside she wanted to curl up. She'd never gone anywhere like that unaccompanied by an adult in her life. And with Janice it was bound to lead to trouble. Hadn't she been in enough trouble now? And where had it got her?

From then on, however, Janice was obsessed with the idea. She never talked about anything else.

'I've checked the map. It's about sixty miles. Easy peasy. An early start. We'll be there midmorning. Get home not too late,' she said.

'Are we talking about a weekend?' Sapphie said, wondering how she'd get away with it.

'Nah. Let's make it a school day. Much more exciting. And it'll be the whole day before they miss us. Easier,' Janice said with a grin.

Sapphie gulped. But there was no stopping Janice. No putting her off now. She was like a steamroller on a roll. And if she did try to put her off, wouldn't Janice turn her back on her? Like Becky. Sapphie'd have no one then.

'It's going to be wicked,' Janice said as the day approached.

Sapphie was still trying to put her off. Didn't think it would ever really happen. She presented Janice regularly with a new problem. 'We can't spend the day in our school uniform,' she said once. 'But we'll have to leave home in school uniform won't we? So what will we do? If we change clothes, what shall we do with our uniform? Where will we change? We can't carry a bag of clothes around with us all day.'

'No problem,' Janice said. 'We'll take some gear with us. Dump the uniform somewhere. Pick it up on the way home. No problem!'

'It'll be an expensive day,' Sapphie said another time.

'I've got every confidence in you,' Janice said. 'And I can chip in. My mum won't miss a few pounds.'

'What do you mean?' Sapphie said. Guessing what she meant, and shocked.

'You can call it borrowing.'

It was no use telling Janice that stealing from her own mother was terrible. It wouldn't make any difference.

'And we'll cut down on the cost hitching a ride,' Janice said.

But that was the bit that worried Sapphie most. There were enough dire warnings about doing things like that. Again, Janice wouldn't be put off though.

'Nothing to it. There'll be two of us. Nobody's going to hurt us, Saph.'

Sapphie wished she could be sure.

'Do you want to do this or do you not?' Janice finally said.

But Janice wouldn't talk to her again if she backed out now.

'Course I want to, Janice,' she said.

'Good on you, Saph,' Janice said. 'It's going to be really cool.'

Sapphie packed some casual clothes into her school bag ready for morning. Then sorted some make-up and shoved it into her bag too. Janice said they needed to look as old as possible. Then she got into bed.

But she couldn't sleep. She was nervous and worried. Frightened in fact. Wondering how she'd let herself get into a situation like this.

When she eventually got to sleep it was a fitful sleep, jolting awake again and again, to worry about the next day.

At least it made a change from worrying about other things.

She woke early and got dressed. Then prowled around her room till it was time to get up.

She went downstairs. Couldn't eat her breakfast. Mum asked her if she was feeling all right. She said yes. Got her bag. Went out and caught a bus to meet Janice.

Janice grabbed Sapphie's arm. 'I can't wait to get there. It's going to be brilliant fun, Saph.'

Janice led Sapphie behind some houses. 'There's some derelict buildings behind here. We can change in there,' she said.

They pushed a creaky door open and went inside. It was dark and dingy and dirty and it smelt. There was evidence of use. Sapphie turned up her nose. She didn't want to look too closely at the debris lying around. Scraps of paper screwed up. Matches. Cigarette butts.

Janice dragged her uniform clothes off. Put on some jeans. A T-shirt. Stuffed her school uniform behind some boxes.

It occurred to Sapphie as she did the same, that it would probably be the last she saw of her school uniform. And how was she going to explain that? But Janice was like a girl possessed.

Next, she pulled a small mirror out of her bag and went to the door.

'Hold this, Saph,' she said and proceeded to slap on some make-up. Then she held the mirror for Sapphie, who did the same. 'Now we're really on our way,' she said. 'We'll walk till we hit the main road, then we'll hitch.'

Janice didn't seem the least put out by any of it. But by the time they came to the main road Sapphie's heart was thumping. And when they eventually selected a spot at the roadside to hitch, her breathing became rapid. Her blood felt like it was churning through her veins, and her head was in a whirl. She thought her legs would give way under her. She took some great heaving gulps of breath as though she were drowning.

Cars whizzed past them. Lorries too. The odd driver stared at them in passing. But most vehicles sped past, ignoring them.

They walked on.

'Don't look so down in the mouth,' Janice said. 'You can't expect it to happen straight away.'

But Sapphie didn't want it to happen at all.

Janice took to veering into the road, dangerously near the cars and lorries as they approached. Making it difficult for the drivers to ignore them. Willing them to stop.

Though when a car did eventually slow down and wait for them, Sapphie was appalled. She watched as if it was all in slow motion. Her mouth twitched and her heart fluttered. Her legs felt like cotton wool.

Janice ran up to the car, dragging Sapphie by the hand.

It was a smart car.

'And where are you two going?' a middle-aged man said as he opened the car door and leaned over to peer at them. He was fat. He had a moustache and hair was sprouting out of his nose. His hair was greasy. He had a smarmy smile on his face.

'Are you going anywhere near Alton Towers?' Janice said breathlessly.

'I can get you a few miles nearer,' he said. 'Hop in.'

'Brilliant,' Janice said.

The man leaned over and opened the front door.

'No. We'll sit in the back,' Janice said. 'It's safer there,' she whispered to Sapphie.

'Please yourself,' the man said.

Janice got in. 'Come on Saph. We're on our way,' she said with a huge grin on her face.

The car pulled away. And as it drove off down the road, Sapphie heard the central lock click.

They were locked in.

As the miles slipped by, Sapphie got more and more distressed.

How could she have been so stupid?

How could she have let Janice talk her into this?

All those warnings about not talking to strangers. All right. They weren't little kids. But they were acting as stupid. Sapphie couldn't believe she was doing this.

The man seemed relaxed enough though. And Janice did too. But Sapphie sat bolt upright on the edge of her seat. Ready to – ready to what?

'How come two young ladies are out on their own then? No school today? No college? No job to go to?'

Sapphie cringed. They didn't look that old.

Janice looked at Sapphie and giggled. 'We've got a day off. Making the most of it. Out on the open road,' she said.

But Sapphie wanted out. She didn't trust this man. She didn't like him.

He'd locked the doors.

'I feel sick,' she suddenly said, her voice a squeak.

The man drove on.

'I'm going to be sick,' Sapphie said. She retched violently.

The man braked so hard they lurched forward and bumped into the front seats. Then he unlocked the central lock. 'Get out!' he yelled. 'I don't want my car ruined.'

Sapphie pushed the door open and almost fell out of the car. For a minute she thought he was going to drive off with Janice, but Janice followed her.

The car pulled away before they had time to pull themselves together.

They sat on the grass verge and Sapphie put her head between her knees.

'What did you want to go and do that for?' Janice yelled.

'He'd locked the doors!' Sapphie wailed.

Janice looked furious. 'So? I don't know about you, but I can look after myself. There are two of us. We could've taken him on between us if he'd tried anything on.'

But Sapphie was just glad to be out of the car. Whatever.

She looked around. They were on the grass verge of a busy dual carriageway, miles from anywhere.

'And now we've got to do it all over again,' Janice complained.

Chapter Ten

'I don't want to do this,' Sapphie gasped. 'Can't we go back, Janice?'

'Lost your nerve?' Janice snapped. 'I might've known you would. Well, whether we go on or back we've got to hitch a ride. So we may as well make it to Alton Towers and be done with it. Are you coming with me or what?'

So they started again. And this time Janice was more aggressive. Shouting names at disappearing cars and lorries. Making rude signs. Shaking her fist at cars as they sped past.

It seemed like nobody wanted to give them a lift.

They plodded along the roadside. Janice getting more and more uptight. Sapphie lost in thought. Thoughts filled with fat smarmy men.

So that when a lorry finally slowed down and stopped, terror welled up in her.

'Come on, Saph,' Janice yelled and ran to catch up with the lorry.

The door opened and Janice clambered up into the cab before the driver had time to ask them where they were going. Sapphie caught up with her and climbed reluctantly up after her, surprised at how high up the door was.

The driver was youngish. With short clipped hair. A goatee beard. And he had some sort of uniform on. Not a bit like the fat man in the car. He made no effort to pull off, but sat staring at them.

'Right, young ladies,' he eventually said. 'So what's it all about then?' It sounded like he wasn't very pleased. 'Where are you going?' he asked.

'Alton Towers,' Janice said. Cheeky in the face of strong vibes of disapproval.

'And how old are you?' he asked next.

'What's this? The third degree?' Janice objected.

'Well it ought to be,' he said. Glancing sideways at them.

'If that's your attitude we'll get out now,' Janice said.

'Oh no you don't,' he said, and pulled out into the road.

Here we go again, Sapphie thought. But Janice looked at her and grinned. 'We'll soon be there at this rate, Saph,' she said.

However, Sapphie couldn't imagine getting anywhere today. She just wished she was back at school.

They drove along the dual carriageway for a while in silence till they came to an island. At which the lorry driver drove all the way round and calmly headed back in the direction they'd come from!

'Hey! We need the other way,' Janice shouted over the sound of the engine.

'I don't think so,' the driver said and continued back down the road.

Suddenly even Janice looked uncertain of herself. 'Stop!' she yelled.

Sapphie was now mute with fear. What was going on? She grabbed hold of Janice's hand and clutched it tightly.

They drove on, back down the road. The persistent drum of the engine the only noise to distract them.

Sapphie wondered whether to try to jump out. But the ground looked such a long way down. And they could fall under a following car and be killed anyway.

Mum! Dad! Sapphie would've done anything to see one of them now. Together. On their own. What did it matter? Either way they'd protect her.

But there was no one here to protect her now. And only her own foolishness had got her here.

She felt sick again.

'I'm going to be sick,' she shouted.

'Hold on,' the lorry driver said. He slowed down. Eventually coming to a stop in a lay-by.

Sapphie didn't know whether to be more afraid than when they were moving or not.

'Are you all right?' the driver said and leaned across to inspect Sapphie. 'You look terrible,' he said.

Sapphie was panting now.

'Take some deep breaths,' he said sympathetically. And then added fiercely, 'You two kids want a good talking to. Do you know how dangerous it is hitching lifts from strangers?'

'That's a bit much coming from you,' Janice snapped.

'You might well say that,' he said. Sounding angrier by the minute. 'Because you're proper messing up my day. Because, actually. I'm taking you back,' he said. 'Back to where you came from. Where did you come from, by the way? You were miles from anywhere when I saw you. I assume you didn't walk there.'

'We got a lift!' Janice said sarcastically. 'And we want to go to Alton Towers. Not back home. Stupid.'

'But I want to go home,' Sapphie said in a small voice.

'Right,' the lorry driver said. 'Some sense at last. So. I'll take you both back as far as I can. To a suitable bus stop. And from there you'll be able to catch a bus back to wherever you came from. Is that a good idea or what?'

Sapphie nodded her head hard. She was so relieved she couldn't find her voice.

But Janice found hers. 'Have you lost it, Sapphie Squires?' she yelled, climbing past her. 'I'm going to Alton Towers with or without you. Let me out, you perv,' she yelled to the lorry driver, who tried to stop her, as she struggled with the door of the lorry.

'You should come back with me,' the driver said insistently.

But Janice wrenched the door open and half fell, half stumbled down out of the lorry. 'We're finished, Sapphie Squires,' she yelled. And rushed off.

Sapphie was numb with relief. Yet terrified for Janice.

'She's a right little spitfire,' the driver said. And started the engine up. 'I did my best. Back we go with you at least.'

He chatted to her on and off. But Sapphie didn't hear what he said. All she could think of was getting back.

He finally dropped her at a bus stop near town. 'Take care,' he called. 'And don't do it again. I hope your mate is all right.'

Sapphie didn't have long to wait for a bus. She was relieved at how normal it felt like to be on a bus.

And she was further relieved to find her clothes where she'd hidden them. She quickly changed back into her school uniform and decided to lie low till after lunch. Though she couldn't wait to get out of the gloomy building and back into the daylight.

She arrived back at school for the afternoon session. Hoping they hadn't noticed her absence all morning.

However, at afternoon registration, Mr Marr eyed her sternly.

'Stay behind, Sapphie,' he said as the others filed off to lessons.

Stephie Peters poked Becky in the ribs. 'I told you, Becks. Off shoplifting again I suppose,' she said.

Becky frowned at Sapphie.

'Where were you this morning?' Mr Marr asked Sapphie when they were alone.

Sapphie couldn't add lies to everything else, so said nothing.

'I rang your mother to check that you should be here,' he said.

Sapphie drew in her breath sharply.

'And she said you should be at school. She's been frantic with worry all morning. I've just rung her to tell her you've arrived safely back at school. And she's on her way here now.'

Then Sapphie broke down and told Mr Marr about Janice's big plans for the day.

Mr Marr looked aghast. 'I don't know what to say to you, Sapphie. After everything else you go and take a risk like this. And where's Janice now?'

Sapphie told her what Janice had done. There was a moment of horrified silence. Then Mr Marr said quietly, 'She could be anywhere.'

The next thing Sapphie knew, her mother had arrived.

When Mr Marr told her about Sapphie's escapade she stared at Sapphie. 'Sapphie,' she said in a harsh whisper. Her face steely. Sapphie had never seen her so angry.

Sapphie dropped her head. 'I'm sorry, Mum,' she said, chewing on her bottom lip.

But Mum's frown deepened. 'That's not good enough, Sapphie,' she said. Her voice cold. 'I can't believe you could be so stupid.'

'I don't think Sapphie will be absconding again,' Mr Marr said. 'I really think she's learned her lesson this time.'

Sapphie threw him a grateful look.

'She won't get the chance again,' Mum said. 'My husband or I will be accompanying our daughter to school every morning from now on, Mr Marr.'

Sapphie knew the problems that would cause them. And felt even worse. 'You needn't worry, Mum,' she whispered. 'It's not necessary.'

'Oh but it is,' her mother said. 'It most certainly is.'

'I think you should both go home now, Mrs Squires,' Mr Marr said. 'Have a good talk. Take it from there. We must hope that Janice gets home all right.'

Back at home Mum laid into Sapphie again. 'Of all the stupid things to do! I don't know what your father will say. We can't trust you anymore, Sapphie,' she said. Then burst into tears herself.

And when Dad came home he was furious with her too.

It was as if their own quarrels were forgotten. And everything that was wrong was now Sapphie's fault.

On her own in her room at last, Sapphie's head was in a whirl. She couldn't see any way of anything coming right anymore.

She hated school now.

And she hated home too.

Her mum and dad hated her. Kate didn't want her. Becky hated her. Even Janice hated her now...

So what could she do about it?

There was only one thing left to do. She'd have to run away!

She frowned. But where to? Where did you run to when you really ran away? She'd only ever done the usual thing and got to the end of the street. But this was for real. She'd got to do it properly.

She tried to think. But her mind was in a panic. She didn't fancy ending up in a cardboard box somewhere.

Then she thought about Gran. And relief flooded her mind.

Gran lived far enough away from all this. She lived on her own. And Gran loved her. She wouldn't turn her away. She'd go to Gran...

It was eight o'clock now.

She could do it right now. Tonight.

Sapphie emptied her money box. She didn't have enough to cover the train fare though. And then she'd need money for a taxi. Gran lived out in the country and there'd be no buses at this time of night.

Mum and Dad were downstairs. Sapphie crept into their bedroom. Dad's wallet lay on his chest of drawers.

Sapphie remembered a time she'd been shocked at Janice 'borrowing' money from her mum. And now here she was stealing from her own father.

She opened the wallet and took out some notes. Then she packed a bag.

Chapter Eleven

She crept down the stairs. She could hear Mum and Dad talking about her. Well now she'd give them something else to talk about.

She closed the door quietly behind her and ran down the road to the bus stop.

It was strange waiting there for a bus in the dark on her own. When a man came and waited alongside her she shied away from him as far away as possible. But he ignored her. It seemed forever till a bus came. But as she got on the bus it was still only eight-forty.

Fifteen minutes later she walked into the station. She looked round anxiously and thought that everyone must be looking at her and wondering what a young girl like her was doing here so late on her own. She went to the ticket office and asked about a train. When they said there was a train at nine-thirty she almost cried with relief. She bought a ticket, then found the right platform and proceeded to watch the screen and listen to the announcements anxiously.

It was all very confusing and she was very tense. Listening and looking round her all the while to confirm that she was in the right place. And when the train drew in still not believing it was the right one. She could end up anywhere if she wasn't sure! It had some of the horrible feeling of the hitching incident about it now. But it wasn't really like that, she told herself. She only had to catch the right train and get to Gran's and everything would be all right this time.

Once she was on the train, however, and heard the correct destinations announced, she began to relax. She liked trains. As it speeded through the countryside it relaxed her more and more. She began to look forward to seeing Gran.

Then she found herself wondering how this had all happened, and found herself thinking back to the night before her birthday. That was when it had all really started. When she became a teenager. Well. She'd known then that things were bad. But she hadn't expected things to take this turn. She'd never expected to find herself on a train speeding through the countryside away from home and her parents.

Sapphie felt as if she'd grown up enough for several years since then, instead of several months.

An hour later she pulled into the station and got out of the train. It was ten-thirty. Not many people got off the train with her. The few who did, rushed off to their cars. Sapphie rushed out of the station and saw a taxi waiting. She'd never felt so relieved before in her life.

Fifteen minutes later she got out of the taxi and walked up to Gran's front door.

And when Gran opened the door she burst into tears.

'Don't ring them!' was the first thing she said when she'd calmed down.

'What do you mean, pet?' Gran said.

'I don't want you to ring Mum and Dad. I don't want them to know where I am,' Sapphie said.

Gran took her into the kitchen. She sat her down and got some milk out of the fridge. Got a mug out of a cupboard. And some cocoa. Mixed it. Put the mug in the microwave. The next thing Sapphie had a steaming mug of hot chocolate in front of her. She put her hands round it and warmed them. They were trembling.

Gran studied Sapphie. 'Let's get you to bed and we'll talk tomorrow,' she said.

Sapphie was so glad. The last thing she wanted to do right now was talk.

For once, she fell fast asleep almost as soon as her head touched the pillow.

When she woke up, at first, she wondered where she was. When she realised, she almost fell out of bed in surprise. She'd actually run away from home.

Gran knocked on the door.

'Are you awake, pet?' she called.

'I'm awake, Gran,' Sapphie said.

Gran came in and sat on the bed.

'Let's get you up and get some breakfast inside you, then we can talk,' she said.

'I want to talk now, Gran,' Sapphie said.

And it all came pouring out...

'Well. You take after your father and that's for sure!' Gran said when Sapphie was finished. 'He got himself into all sorts of pickles when he was your age.' She patted Sapphie's hand.

'Did he?' Sapphie said. 'Did he, Gran? I thought you'd be shocked,' she said sheepishly. She wasn't exactly proud of the things she'd told Gran.

'I suppose you only did what you thought was best,

pet,' Gran said with a deep sigh. 'And it all got out of hand.' She got up and fussed with some things around the room. 'I rang them, by the way,' she said. Her back to Sapphie.

Sapphie was suddenly angry. 'I didn't want them to know where I was, Gran,' she said. 'There's no point in my running away if they know where I am. I wanted them to be worried.'

'But they were frantic, pet. Still are. I *had* to ring them.' She sat down on the bed again. 'Otherwise they'd be ringing the police. Thinking the worst. We had to let them know you're all right at least.'

'Well, I'm not going back, Gran,' Sapphie said. 'I'm going to stay here. They don't want me. Kate doesn't want me. I can stay here can't I, Gran?'

Gran clutched Sapphie's hand. 'You can stay as long as you like, pet,' she said. Then she grabbed hold of Sapphie and hugged her tight. 'But you're wrong about them not wanting you,' she whispered into Sapphie's hair.

Gran watched Sapphie eat a bowl of steaming porridge.

'I don't want them to get divorced, Gran,' Sapphie eventually said.

'I know, my pet. I'm sad about it too. Nobody's more sad about it than me,' she said.

'And I've got to choose which one of them to live with,' Sapphie said.

Gran got up and put the bowls in the sink. Cut some thick slices of brown nutty bread and dropped them into the toaster. 'It's the only thing they can do. It's not really a choice they can make for you at your age. But whichever one you live with,' she said slowly, 'you'll see plenty of the other. They'll both of them still be your parents, you know. And they'll both still love you. It's their own relationship they've got to sort out, Sapphie. Not yours.'

'That's what Kate said,' Sapphie said. 'But it still affects me. It's not fair, Gran.'

'Of course it affects you, pet,' Gran said. 'But life's like that. You've played *Consequences* haven't you?'

Gran got the toast out of the toaster. Buttered a slice thickly for herself. Passed the other slice to Sapphie. 'How many of the kids at your school come from divorced families?' she said, spreading honey on her toast.

'I don't know. Lots,' Sapphie said.

'And they're all right, aren't they? They've not got two heads or anything.'

Sapphie giggled.

'That's better pet. I've not seen you smile since you got here.'

Later, she helped Gran cut the grass. Then they weeded the borders together.

'Feeling better?' Gran said when they stopped for a drink of home-made lemonade.

Sapphie nodded her head.

In the next few days she was aware that Gran talked regularly to Mum and Dad. But she didn't talk to them. Not yet.

Then, after a few more days, she knew that she couldn't stay here forever. And part of her now wanted to go home. They'd got to get everything sorted out once and for all.

Eventually, it was Dad who came for her.

When they got home he patted the sofa. She sat down next to him and snuggled up to him.

'What are we going to do about this mess?' he said hoarsely.

Sapphie buried her head in his side.

'This – splitting up—' he said. 'We're not doing it lightly, you know. But we can't live together any longer, Sapphie. Mum and me,' he added, as if it needed to be said.

Sapphie struggled again to understand. 'Is it something to do with Max?' she asked.

She felt Dad tense. 'It doesn't help, them being such good friends,' he said. His voice betraying his jealousy. 'But Mum and me. We're two different people from the two who once made each other happy, Saph.' He hugged her hard. 'About the only thing we feel the same about is the way we both love you. That will never change.' His voice shook with emotion now. 'We just can't make each other happy any more, Saph.' He sighed a long sigh. 'And if it wasn't for you we'd have called it a day long ago. But now it's got to stop.' He drew apart from Sapphie and looked into her eyes. 'We've got to get you back to school. And then I'll be moving out. As soon as I can find a flat, pet. And it's best you stay with Mum. Eh?'

Sapphie began to cry.

That night, again, she couldn't sleep.

Chapter Twelve

The school secretary ushered her and Mum and Dad into the studio. This time, there were more chairs. And more people.

Mr Marr. Miss Marriott. The headmaster too. And also someone who introduced herself as the educational psychologist. Sapphie felt intimidated just by the title.

Her parents looked crestfallen as they sat down. Sapphie felt – threatened.

There was the same rigmarole as before. Coffees all round.

When they finally got going, Sapphie let it all go over her head. She was exhausted from lack of sleep. Couldn't focus on anything that was being said. So let them get on with it.

Conversation was brisk and businesslike. As if they were discussing a business project.

But then the headmaster addressed Sapphie directly.

'From now on, Sapphie,' he said, pausing. Waiting till he had her full attention. Unwillingly, she looked up at him. 'From now on, if for any reason you are missing from school at any time, your parents will be informed straight away.' Her parents nodded their heads in agreement. 'And you will have to get signed in to each lesson.' Her form teacher nodded this time. 'And for the foreseeable future, there will be a weekly review meeting to discuss your work and your behaviour.' He waited for Sapphie to acknowledge what he'd said. She did so with a frown and a slight nod. 'In the meantime I'm asking Miss Pringle, our educational psychologist, to do a report, Sapphie.'

The educational psychologist smiled at Sapphie. But Sapphie didn't want to be tested by any educational psychologist, and avoided her eyes.

Then the headmaster told her that she must keep away from Janice. 'And Janice will be told to keep away from you.'

Sapphie didn't think that was a problem. She hadn't spoken to Janice since that day. It was rumoured round the class that Janice had got to Alton Towers. But Sapphie wasn't interested in finding out any more than that.

The only thing of interest to her right now was that she felt like she must be one of the worst students in the school.

Later that week, they told her that Dad had finally found a flat.

'It's a nice flat,' Mum said. 'And it's only a few miles away.' She smiled a falsely cheerful smile.

'I'll be leaving tomorrow, darling.' Dad said. 'But there's a spare bedroom there for you. You'll be able to come and see me often.'

'A few miles away. It may as well be a hundred!' wailed Sapphie.

The next morning they got up as normal. Had breakfast as normal. But nothing was really normal about today.

Today was the last time her dad would have breakfast with them.

Today was the last time he'd be here in this house with them.

Today was the last time they were a family together.

When he was ready to go, Dad dropped a light kiss on her cheek. She grabbed him. 'Don't go, Dad,' she spluttered.

But after sending her an anguished look he grabbed his bag and walked quickly out of the door.

Mum looked ready to cry too.

So if this was making them both so unhappy, why were they doing it? Sapphie still didn't get it.

She was used to getting home to an empty house. But today when she got home from school, the house felt deserted. Always, before, they were both coming back. But today, one of them wasn't. Her dad would never come home again. It felt like the house knew and was sad.

She wandered round. Went into her parents' bedroom. Opened Dad's wardrobe. His things weren't there. She could smell his aftershave though. She sat on the bed and her body slumped. She couldn't even cry.

She waited anxiously for Mum to come home.

When she arrived, Mum seemed lost as well. She, too, wandered round the house from room to room just like Sapphie had. Was she looking in his wardrobe too, Sapphie wondered?

Mum laid three places for supper. And blushed. She took the third knife and fork away quickly.

They ate in silence.

Dad's absence was palpable.

This is what it's going to be like from now on, Sapphie thought. She left the table and rushed up to her bedroom. Flung herself on the bed. This time the tears came.

Mum came after her, but she didn't say anything. Perhaps she didn't know what to say. They held each other tight.

The rest of that week, it was the same. The house didn't feel right any more. It wasn't something she could explain. It was the same house she'd always lived in but it didn't feel the same. It felt – demeaned. Less like home than it was before. Sapphie began to wish she and Mum had been the ones to move out. And yet. Wouldn't that have been even worse?

On Saturday morning, she got ready to visit Dad. But the thought was no comfort. She didn't want to be just a visitor. *Visiting* her dad for goodness sake! It was obscene.

Mum drove her to the new development of flats on the edge of town. She got out of the car with her.

Sapphie looked around. It was a large building. In your face. It couldn't be more different from their own mellow house standing back off the road with the drive up to it. Windows stared at her. The entrance was intimidating. She wondered which window Dad was behind.

Mum walked her up a newly landscaped walkway and they stopped at the entrance door. She scanned the intercom and buzzed.

Sapphie heard Dad's voice on the intercom. 'I'll come down,' he said. His voice terse.

Mum turned to leave Sapphie there. 'I won't come in with you, darling,' she said. Also terse. 'Have a good time. See you tomorrow.' She walked off.

What was Mum going to do this weekend? Sapphie wondered. Would she miss her? It was Mum's turn to be lonely now. In this new set-up it seemed that one or other of them was always doomed to be lonely.

The door opened and Dad stood there. He grabbed her bag and hugged her self-consciously. 'Welcome,' he said, and led her up a communal staircase on to a landing. 'Here we are,' he said, pointing to an open door.

It was a nice living room. Big. Light. Sparsely furnished. His computer sat on a large desk which was already covered with paperwork.

He took her over to the window. 'It's a nice view up here,' he said. Polite. And far too restrained. Her dad usually swept her off her feet. And where was the cheeky grin?

Sapphie soon saw that the grin had been replaced by melancholy puppy-dog eyes that followed her round.

'Come and look at your bedroom,' he said anxiously. And took her to an almost empty room. Basically there was just a bed. 'This will be your room, Sapphie. It will be just like your bedroom at home. I want you to tell me how you want it doing up,' he said. 'We'll go and choose some colours eh? Then I'll paint it. And we'll buy some furniture together.'

So later, they went into town to choose paint. And buy some furniture. She chose a unit that would double as a desk and dressing table, and some drawers. They bought a mirror. Some shelves. 'I'll put them up for you next week,' he said.

Next week.

When she wouldn't be there.

All day Dad was painfully anxious to please her, making Sapphie feel uncomfortable. And when he cooked supper for them that evening, he looked pathetic. He'd often done the cooking at home – spreading himself about and messing up all the space in their large kitchen. Here, in this flat, moving carefully around in the tiny kitchen, he looked pitiful.

Eating their meal they didn't have much to say to each other.

Was this how it was going to be from now on?

Even when they settled down for the evening, conversation was stilted. They watched TV. It was rubbish. And when she could stay up indefinitely, Sapphie chose to go to bed early. Then she lay listening to the unfamiliar sounds from the building around her and couldn't sleep. The sound of the traffic disturbed her. There was a light outside. It kept her awake.

She wondered if Dad was asleep next door. How was he feeling? How did he feel every night in this flat on his own? He must be very lonely.

She lay awake for most of the night.

The next day he took her to the cinema. Was this what it was going to be like? Finding things to do to avoid facing up to the fact that there was this empty hole inside both of them.

When the weekend was over and it was time to leave, it was the same as when she'd arrived – only in reverse. Dad delivered her home. Stayed outside. Both her parents looking beside themselves with unhappiness. Dad leaving. Sad puppy-dog eyes.

Sapphie felt crushed. She went straight up to her bedroom.

When Mum followed her up, Sapphie couldn't contain herself any longer. 'You said it would be all right, Mum!' she said accusingly. 'But it was awful. It was like we were strangers. It was even worse than I thought it would be.'

'It's been very quiet here,' Mum said as if she hadn't heard a word that Sapphie said. Immersed in her own feelings. 'I've missed you. Weekends are going to be very strange from now on. Not getting to do any of the things we used to do together,' she rambled on. Her eyes were dull. 'I just get to see you at the business side of the week now. It's strange.'

The next problem raised itself when Mum had to go away on business. And it was decided that Sapphie would sleep at Kate's. Dad's hours being so unreasonable and his flat not finished yet. But Sapphie hadn't seen much of Kate recently. And she'd never slept there before.

When she got there it was a bit like the visit to Dad's at first. A bit stilted.

Kate prepared a lovely supper as usual. Pasta with

spicy aubergines, tomatoes, basil and parmesan. That bit was fine.

It was when they'd finished loading the dishwasher and tidied the kitchen that things got bad again.

Suddenly everything in Sapphie's life was awkward. And she'd had enough of it. She flounced off to her bedroom.

But Kate rushed after her.

'I know you're hurting, pet,' she said.

'I'm not your pet,' Sapphie said.

'All right. I know you're hurting, *Sapphie*,' Kate said.

Sapphie couldn't resist a little smile.

Kate leaned over and lifted Sapphie's chin up so she could look into her eyes. 'I'm still your friend, Sapphie. Always will be,' she said. And smiled at her. Kate had a lovely smile.

Things were better then.

They went back into the sitting room. There was nothing on TV, but Kate had got a video out for them.

'At the weekend Dad and I just sat staring at the box. It was awful, Kate,' Sapphie said.

'It will get better,' Kate said. 'This is just a stage. Everybody getting used to things. Adjusting. It will be all right soon.'

Sapphie sighed. 'Mum keeps saying that too. But Dad was like this stranger,' she insisted. 'And Mum's odd too. I think she was lonely while I was away.'

'Everything will get better. Cross my heart and hope to die,' Kate said. 'I'll arrange some outings with your mum at the weekend. Girls' days out. She'll be all right. And another couple of visits to your dad and you'll feel at home there. You'll all be back to your old selves soon.'

Sapphie wished she could believe her.

At school, Sapphie had no friends now. She never talked to Janice any more. But sometimes Becky stared at her. And Sapphie wondered what she was thinking.

Suddenly, this *apartness*, like she'd felt at Dad's – there with him but not part of his life – took a grip of Sapphie. She felt apart from everyone. Isolated. Like she was in a world of her own. The teachers' voices sounded at a distance. As if they weren't talking to her. They were talking to the others. But not to her. The kids were talking to each other. But not to her.

The feeling settled in the pit of Sapphie's stomach. Like a dread. And she didn't know what of. She went to bed feeling this dread gripping her. It was there when she woke up. It was there when she went to school. And when she got home.

She was permanently tired.

She'd never felt so miserable and lonely in her life.

At home, Mum was distracted.

At school they continued to ignore her. It didn't matter not talking to Janice. She'd never really liked Janice anyway. But Sapphie often looked longingly at Becky when Becky wasn't looking.

Her work dropped off even more now. The reasons it had dropped off before had been of her own making. But now, she couldn't help herself. She couldn't concentrate. And nothing she did came out right.

She began to feel sick at the thought of school. Especially last thing at night and first thing in the mornings.

One morning she clutched her stomach and told Mum she felt too sick to go to school. So Mum let her stay home. And the next morning it was the same. And the next.

This not-going-to-school felt a bit like truanting. But it wasn't like the other times. This was something she couldn't help. It was like being ill but not being ill. And not knowing what the matter was.

Mum dragged her to the doctor, but Sapphie couldn't tell him what the matter was. The doctor said something vague about giving it time.

Was that all they could come up with? Sapphie thought.

According to all adults, it seemed that with *time* everything would be all right.

Except that they were all wrong. Things just kept getting worse, didn't they?

Chapter Thirteen

It was Becky eventually got her out of it.

While the others gave her the cold shoulder, Becky started to smile occasionally at Sapphie again. And those smiles meant so much to her.

Then one day she took Sapphie's arm in the dinner queue. And when Sapphie smiled back gratefully at her, Becky squeezed her arm.

But when she turned up at home one day after school when Sapphie had been too sick to go, her heart lurched.

'I thought I'd call,' she said. 'Seeing as you're poorly.'

Sapphie took Becky up to her bedroom and they sat on the floor cushions shyly.

Sapphie put a CD on.

Then they began to talk.

And once Sapphie had started talking, she couldn't stop. It poured out of her like a stream. She talked and talked and then talked some more. About both her parents seeming like strangers at the moment. About Kate not wanting her to live with her. About the truanting. It was the first time she'd talked to anybody about that properly. About how Janice's shoplifting had made her feel as if she'd done it herself. Then the aborted trip to Alton Towers. 'I didn't even want to go, Becky. Yet I went along with it. What does that make me?' About the lifts they'd hitched. 'It was awful,' she said, knowing that words didn't convey how bad it had really been. She told Becky about the first sleazeball who'd given them a lift. And the second man who turned out to be A-OK. 'If he hadn't brought me back, Becky, goodness knows what might have happened.' And when she told Becky about running away to Gran's, Becky's eyebrows shot skywards. 'Wow!' she said.

The flow dried up at last and Sapphie smiled shyly at Becky. 'I'm so glad you came round,' she said.

'Same here,' Becky said. 'I've missed you Sapphie.'

They smiled a shy familiar smile at each other.

'What about Stephie Peters?' Sapphie said.

'She's all right,' Becky said. 'I like her. But *you're* my best friend.'

The next day, Sapphie went to school. And at last things *were* better. More normal than they'd been for such a long while. She stuck to Becky like a limpet all day. And Stephie Peters went around with her old friends.

And after school, when she went home with Becky, it was better there, too. There was the same coming and going. The same squabbling. Becky's mum acting as referee. And this time it felt all right.

Another weekend came round. And another visit to Dad. Which Sapphie was dreading and looking forward to at the same time.

'It's not fair really,' Mum said. 'Dad has you for the best part of the week. The house is very quiet now at the weekend.' But then she brightened up. 'Kate rang last night, though. We're going out today,' she said. 'Having a fun day out in town. And tomorrow I'm going out with Max,' she added quietly.

Sapphie stared at Mum.

This time when she arrived at Dad's he almost pulled her through the door in his eagerness. Then he grinned at her.

It was such a relief to see that grin again.

'Come and see,' he said and took her straight through to her bedroom. He'd painted the walls the pale lilac she'd chosen. And painted the floor cream like she'd said.

Sapphie admired it. 'We'll buy a rug this weekend,' he told her. 'I want this room to be just as special as your bedroom at home.' Sapphie grinned too. It was so good to see him so enthusiastic about something again. 'What about the shelves? Do you like them?' he said. She nodded. 'I thought you could bring a few of your things from home and arrange them on them. Or we could buy some new things for you,' he said.

'No, I'd like to bring some of my things from home next time,' she said. 'That will be good, Dad.'

Then Dad took her onto his tiny pocket-handkerchief-sized-balcony. 'I want to do something with this next, Sapphie. Get some plants,' he said. 'Some tubs. Shall we go to the garden centre and get some this afternoon?'

So that afternoon they went to the garden centre. Treated themselves to tea and cakes. Overdid the buying bit and came back loaded with plants. 'Will we find room for all of them?' Dad said.

They both giggled.

So things were better here as well.

She liked her room now. And she'd enjoyed helping Dad with the plants. Then she helped him cook supper. Chattering while they worked. It was almost like old times.

And when Dad took her home, this time Mum asked him in. She made them a drink. And the three of them sat round the kitchen table.

'Did you have a good weekend?' Mum asked.

'Yes,' Sapphie said.

'It was good,' Dad said. 'You?'

Sapphie thought about Max and held her breath. Were they going to start quarrelling again?

But Mum just smiled too. 'Good,' she said.

Sapphie reflected that it wasn't exactly like when they were together, but Mum and Dad were talking instead of quarrelling.

And when Dad had gone, Mum told Sapphie all about her weekend. And this time, when Sapphie told Mum about hers, Mum listened attentively.

'Perhaps things *are* going to be all right now, Mum!' Sapphie suddenly said. And hardly dared believe it, but it was true.

Her mum laughed. 'I never thought I'd hear *you* say that!' she said.

Sapphie laughed too.

'It's good to hear you laughing, Sapphie,' Mum said.

And hugged her tight. 'We're all going to get through this, pet. You see.'

And for once Sapphie believed her. Because it had already begun to happen.